P9-DWS-960

Dear Parent:
Your child's love of reading starts here!

Every child learns to read in a different way and at his or her own speed. You can help your young reader improve and become more confident by encouraging his or her own interests and abilities. You can also guide your child's spiritual development by reading stories with biblical values and Bible stories, like I Can Read! books published by Zonderkidz. From books your child reads with you to the first books he or she reads alone, there are I Can Read! books for every stage of reading:

SHARED READING
Basic language, word repetition, and whimsical illustrations, ideal for sharing with your emergent reader.

BEGINNING READING
Short sentences, familiar words, and simple concepts for children eager to read on their own.

READING WITH HELP
Engaging stories, longer sentences, and language play for developing readers.

READING ALONE
Complex plots, challenging vocabulary, and high-interest topics for the independent reader.

ADVANCED READING
Short paragraphs, chapters, and exciting themes for the perfect bridge to chapter books.

I Can Read! books have introduced children to the joy of reading since 1957. Featuring award-winning authors and illustrators and a fabulous cast of beloved characters, I Can Read! books set the standard for beginning readers.

A lifetime of discovery begins with the magical words **"I Can Read!"**

Visit www.icanread.com for information on enriching your child's reading experience.
Visit www.zonderkidz.com for more Zonderkidz I Can Read! titles.

Be strong and courageous. Do not be afraid
or terrified because of them, for the LORD
your God goes with you; he will never leave
you nor forsake you.
—*Deuteronomy 31:6*

ZONDERKIDZ

The Princess Twins Collection
Copyright © 2017 by Mona Hodgson
Illustrations © 2017 Julie Olson

Requests for information should be addressed to:

Zonderkidz, 3900 Sparks Dr. SE, Grand Rapids, Michigan 49546

ISBN 978-0-310-75319-3 (hardcover)

The Princess Twins and the Puppy ISBN 978-0-310-75064-2 (2015)
The Princess Twins Play in the Garden ISBN 978-0-310-75050-5 (2015)
The Princess Twins and the Birthday Party ISBN 978-0-310-75067-3 (2016)
The Princess Twins and the Tea Party ISBN 978-0-310-75038-3 (2016)

Design: Diane Mielke

Printed in China

17 18 19 20 21 22 23 24 25 /DSC/ 13 14 15 12 11 10 9 8 7 6 5 4 3 2 1

ZONDERkidz

I Can Read!

BEGINNING 1 READING

The Princess Twins
and the Puppy

Story by Mona Hodgson
Pictures by Julie Olson

Princess Abby and her sister, Emma,
sipped tea in the garden.

Tickle. Tickle.

Something tickled Abby's leg.

Abby giggled and she wiggled.

Tickle. Tickle.

Abby looked under the table.

Puppy barked and jumped.

"It's not playtime,"

Emma told Puppy.

Tickle. Tickle.

"Shoo." Abby clapped her hands.

Puppy ran out of the garden.

Abby and Emma finished their tea.

Now it was playtime.

"Puppy," Princess Abby called.

"Puppy," called Princess Emma.

Puppy didn't come.

"Maybe Puppy ran up the tower,"
said Abby.

14

The princesses looked in the tower,
but they didn't find Puppy.

Abby opened the castle door.

"Puppy," she called.

Abby looked in Puppy's bed,

but she didn't find Puppy.

"Puppy," Princess Emma called.

Emma looked in her bedroom,
but she didn't find Puppy.

"Puppy," Princess Abby called.

She looked in the library,

but she didn't find Puppy.

Emma stopped at a closed door.

"What if Puppy is in the basement?"

she asked.

"Puppy," Abby called.

"Woof. Woof," said Puppy.

Princess Abby and Princess Emma

looked into the basement.

"Puppy!" they called.

Puppy didn't come.

"Woof. Woof," said Puppy.

"Puppy needs us," said Abby.

"I'm not going down there,"

Emma said.

Abby was afraid of the dark.

Abby had to be very brave.

"Jesus, help me be brave,"

prayed Abby.

Abby took a lantern.

She tiptoed down the stairs.

Abby's knees shook.

"Jesus is with me," she said.

"Woof. Woof," said Puppy.

Abby found Puppy stuck in a box.

Tickle. Tickle.

Abby tickled Puppy's chin.

"Thank you, Jesus, for making
me brave," prayed Abby.

Abby carried Puppy upstairs.

Puppy woofed and wiggled.

Now it really was playtime.

People look at the outward appearance, but the
LORD looks at the heart.
—*1 Samuel 16:7*

I Can Read! BEGINNING READING 1

The Princess Twins
Play in the Garden

Story by Mona Hodgson
Pictures by Julie Olson

Princess Emma and Princess Abby
walked in the castle garden.

"God made this a lovely day,"

Princess Abby said to her sister.

Emma stopped and screamed.

"There's a bug on my pretty dress."

"It will get my dress dirty.

Get it off me!" Emma said.

Abby gently lifted the ladybug

and set it on a rose.

"Thank you," said Emma.

Abby and Emma saw their friends.

"It's time for our playdate,"

said Abby.

Princess Abby ran down the hill.

Princess Emma walked down the hill.

She didn't want her dress

to get dirty.

She wanted to look pretty.

43

"Have fun at the castle,"
said Mrs. Lee.
She waved good-bye
to her children.

"Let's play in the garden,"

said Princess Abby.

The children ran up the hill

to the castle.

"We can have tea," said Emma.

"I don't want to get dirty."

The children had a tea party

in the garden.

Abby gave her friends rides
on her pony.

Emma sat in a chair and watched.

"A princess must look pretty,"

Emma said.

Abby and her friends

made sand castles.

The children played soccer

with Princess Abby.

A muddy ball hit Emma's dress.

"How could you?" she said

to her friend who'd kicked it.

Tears filled the girl's eyes.

"I'm sorry," she said.

Emma was sorry she'd yelled.

"That's okay," she said.

Emma hugged her friend.

"Let's play," said Emma.

She kicked the soccer ball.

Mrs. Lee waved.

It was time to go home.

Emma and Abby ran down the hill
with the children.

"Mama, we had lots of fun,"
said the children.

Mrs. Lee smiled at the princesses.

"Thank you," she said.

"You are both lovely girls."

A ladybug landed on Emma's dress.

She smiled and prayed,

"Thank you, God, for a lovely day."

Be kind and compassionate
to one another.
—*Ephesians 4:32*

ZONDERkidz

I Can Read!

BEGINNING
1
READING

The Princess Twins
and the Birthday Party

Story by Mona Hodgson
Pictures by Julie Olson

67

Princess Emma's eyes popped open.

Emma jumped out of bed.

"Today is our birthday!"

Princess Abby jumped up.

"Happy Birthday, Emma."

Emma hugged her twin sister.

"Happy Birthday to you too."

The princesses picked out

their prettiest dresses.

Emma and Abby pinned up their hair.

They put pretty crowns
on their heads.

"We're ready for our special day,"

said Princess Emma.

Princess Emma and Princess Abby

walked down the stairs.

Emma and Abby ate pancakes
and drank apple juice.

"It's almost time for our party,"
Emma said.

Emma twirled.

"You look beautiful," said the queen.

"You are even more beautiful inside.

God sees your heart," said the king.

"He sees you are loving and kind."

Later Emma and Abby

made pretty name cards.

They put them next to the tea cups.

There was a place for each friend.

The castle bell rang.

The princesses ran to the door.

They said hello to each girl.

Emma looked at her friends,

but she didn't see Beth.

"Where's Beth?" she asked.

"She left," said one of the girls.

Emma looked outside.

She saw Beth down the path.

"Beth, wait," said Emma.

She ran to catch up with her friend.

"What's wrong?" asked Emma.

"My dress is too plain," Beth said.
Emma didn't want Beth to miss the
party.

"I know what you need," said Emma.

She took the crown off her head.

Emma set the crown on Beth's head.

Beth twirled.

"I feel beautiful," she said.

"Thank you for your kindness."

"You are beautiful," said Emma.

"And you are even more beautiful inside."

The girls ran back to the party.

He [God] gives grace to those
who are not proud.
—*Proverbs 3:34*

I Can Read!™

The Princess Twins and the Tea Party

Story by Mona Hodgson / Pictures by Julie Olson

99

Princess Emma dressed up.

Today was the Spring Tea.

Emma wanted everything
to be perfect.

She ran to the castle kitchen.

The cook was making the cakes.

"Did you remember the sugar?"

Emma asked.

The cook stopped stirring.

"Of course I added the sugar,"

he said.

"I just want things to taste right,"
said Emma.

"They will taste good,"

the cook said.

Emma ran to the tea room.

The table looked pretty,

but the napkins didn't look right.

Emma unfolded them.

Then she folded them her way.

Puppy ran into the tea room.

"You don't belong in here,"

said Emma.

"You could ruin the tea party."

She picked up Puppy

and set him outside.

Emma went back to the tea room.

Where were the name cards?

Where was her sister Abby?

Emma ran to find her sister.

She ran right into Abby.

The name cards flew to the floor.

"Now we have to make new cards,"
said Emma.

Abby picked up the cards.

"There's nothing wrong with these,"

she said.

"I want everything to be perfect,"

said Emma.

"Only God is perfect," Abby said.

Abby set the name cards by the cups.

"Don't worry, Emma.

Just enjoy the party," said Abby.

The castle bell rang.

The princesses ran to the door.

Princess Emma and Princess Abby

took their friends to the tea room.

Everything was perfect.

Then Emma saw Puppy by the table.

She tried to grab Puppy.

Instead, Emma stepped on his tail.

Puppy wiggled. Emma wobbled.

Then Emma bumped the table.

The table tumbled to the floor.

Tea splashed in a puddle.

Puppy slurped tea.

"Welcome to Puppy's perfect party,"

said Abby.

Emma giggled.

The other girls giggled too.

Then they enjoyed sweet tea

and yummy applesauce cake.